BY CORI BROOKE

art by Katie Alexander

THIS
BOY
CAN!

FIVE MILE

This boy protects and treats animals well,

This boy teaches kids how to add up and spell,

This boy sings proudly for everyone to hear,

This boy writes plays — he's a total Shakespeare.

This boy seeks equality for women and men,

This boy teaches mindfulness — he's chill and zen,

This boy helps women birth babies as a midwife nurse,

This boy loves rhyming words, and writes poems in verse.

This boy designs gowns of elegant shape and fit,

This boy plays the harp in the orchestra pit,

These boys are sensitive, caring and smart.

They did what they loved
And they followed their hearts.

This boy adores books – and reads for hours and hours,

This boy creates lovely arrangements with flowers,

This boy knows kindness matters and helps people in need,

This boy volunteers to help others succeed.

This boy stands up to bullies and sticks by his mates,

This boy wears tights and dances on skates,

This boy stays home with his daughter and son,

This boy is perfecting his Grandma's won ton.

This boy creates beautiful pieces of art,

This boy is proud of being super smart.

These boys are all sensitive, caring and smart.
They did what they loved,
And followed their hearts.

Look in the mirror.

Ask: "What can this boy do?"

You can do what you love,

What you really want to.

There is no limit to what you can achieve,

If you work
hard, and truly
believe.

What you love to do is what you can become,
So never let anyone say what you love is dumb.
If it makes you happy and makes your heart sing,
Then that is a wonderful, special thing.

Celebrate your differences, be tall and be proud,
Don't worry about being in the so-called in-crowd.
Because you're also sensitive, caring and smart,
You must do what you love
And follow your heart.

FIVE MILE

Five Mile, the publishing division of Regency Media

www.fivemile.com.au

First published 2020

Written by Cori Brooke
Illustrations by Katie Alexander
Text copyright © Cori Brooke, 2020
Illustration copyright ©Katie Alexander, 2020

ISBN: 978-1-92238-524-6 (hbk)

Printed in China 5 4 3 2

NATIONAL LIBRARY OF AUSTRALIA

A catalogue record for this book is available from the National Library of Australia